If You Take a Mouse to the Movies

If You Take a

BY **Laura Numeroff**

ILLUSTRATED BY **Felicia Bond**

▦ A Laura Geringer Book

An Imprint of HarperCollins*Publishers*

Mouse to the Movies

If You Take a Mouse to the Movies
Text copyright © 2000 by Laura Numeroff
Illustrations copyright © 2000 by Felicia Bond
Printed in the U.S.A. All rights reserved.
www.harperchildrens.com
Library of Congress Cataloging-in-Publication Data
Numeroff, Laura Joffe.
If you take a mouse to the movies / by Laura
Numeroff ; illustrated by Felicia Bond.
p.   cm.
Summary: Taking a mouse to the movies can
lead to letting him do other things, such as
making a snowman, listening to Christmas
carols, and decorating the Christmas tree.
ISBN 0-06-027868-4 (lib. bdg.) ISBN 0-06-027867-6
[1. Mice—Fiction. 2. Christmas—Fiction.]
I. Bond, Felicia, ill. II. Title.
PZ7.N964Ij 2000   99-27258
[E]—DC21   CIP
                                                      AC

5 6 7 8 9 10 ❖

NOW SHOWING

If you take a mouse to the movies,

he'll ask you for some popcorn.

When you give him the popcorn,

he'll want to string it all together.

Then he'll want to hang it on a Christmas tree.

You'll have to buy him one.

On the way home, he'll see a
snowman in your neighbor's yard.
He'll want to make one of his own.

Then he'll need a carrot for a nose.

When he's all finished, he'll decide to build a fort.
He'll ask you to help him.

Then he'll want to make
some snowballs and have
a snowball fight.

Playing outside will make him cold.
He'll want to go inside and curl up on the couch.

He'll ask you for a blanket.

Once he's nice and cozy,
he'll want to listen to Christmas carols.

You'll have to find some on the radio.

He'll probably sing along.

The carols will remind him of his Christmas tree,
so he'll want to make ornaments.

You'll get him some paper and glue.

He'll ask you for glitter.

When the ornaments are done,

he'll hang them all up.

Then he'll stand back
to look at the tree.

He'll notice his popcorn string is missing!

So he'll want to make another one.

He'll ask you for some popcorn.

And chances are,
when you give him the popcorn,

he'll want you to take him to the movies.

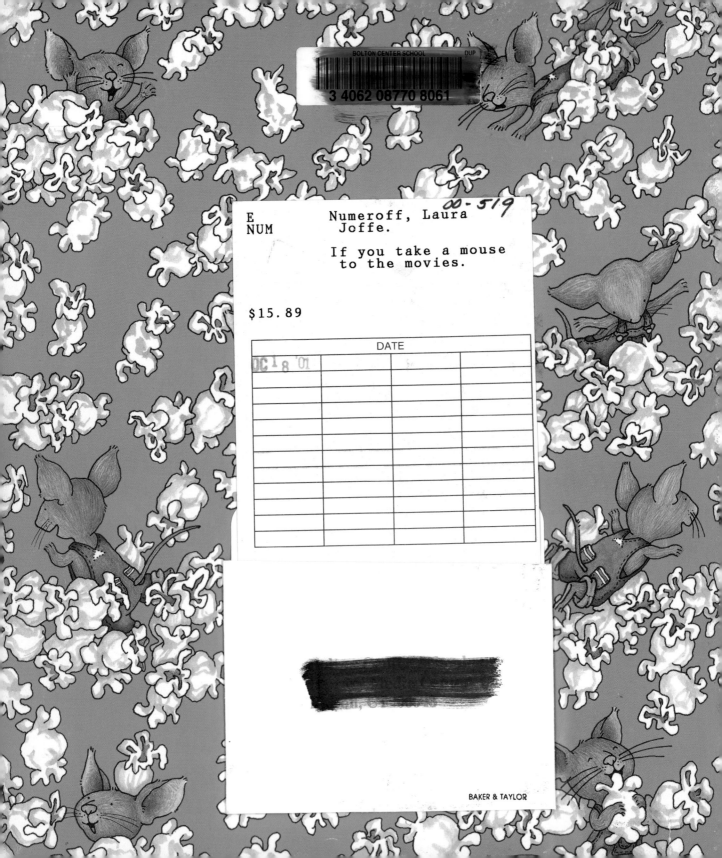

00-519

E
NUM

Numeroff, Laura
   Joffe.

If you take a mouse
to the movies.

$15.89

DATE			
DC 18 '01			